# this book belongs to:

a gift from:

page ahead
children's literacy program
www.pageahead.org

# MY LITTLE SISTER HUGGED AN APE

WRITTEN BY
## BILL GROSSMAN

ILLUSTRATED BY
## KEVIN HAWKES

**Dragonfly Books®**
New York

To Gail—B.G.

For Grace—K.H.

Published by
Dragonfly Books
an imprint of
Random House Children's Books
a division of Random House, Inc.
New York

Dragonfly Books and colophon are registered trademarks of Random House, Inc.
Visit us on the Web! www.randomhouse.com/kids
Educators and librarians, for a variety of teaching tools, visit us at www.randomhouse.com/teachers
The Library of Congress has catalogued the hardcover edition of this work as follows:
Grossman, Bill.
My little sister hugged an ape / Bill Grossman ; illustrated by Kevin Hawkes.
p.  cm.
Summary: Little sister is on a hugging spree, out to hug a different animal for every letter of the alphabet.
ISBN: 978-0-517-80017-1 (hardcover)—ISBN: 978-0-517-80018-8 (lib. bdg.)
[1. Hugging—Fiction. 2. Sisters—Fiction. 3. Alphabet. 4. Stories in rhyme.] I. Hawkes, Kevin, ill. II. Title.
PZ8.3.G914Mp 2004    [E]—dc22  2003018787
ISBN: 978-0-385-73660-2 (pbk.)
Reprinted by arrangement with Alfred A. Knopf Books for Young Readers
MANUFACTURED IN CHINA
October 2008
10  9  8  7  6  5  4  3  2  1

First Dragonfly Books Edition

My little sister hugged an APE
And squeezed its tummy out of shape,
Till it let out a burp with a horrible sound
That knocked my poor sister right onto the ground.

My little sister hugged a BUG,
A mighty tiny thing to hug.
It slipped from her arms and flew up her nose.
Bugs prefer noses to arms, I suppose.

My little sister hugged a COW
But must have hugged it wrong somehow.
It squirted its milk all over the place,
Soaking my sister's whole body and face.

My little sister hugged a DEER,
But one of its horns got stuck in her ear.
And she hung from the deer like a coat on a rack,
Till the deer tipped its head and she fell on her back.

My little sister hugged an EEL.
She liked its slippery, slimy feel.
It tied itself up in a long, icky knot
And hung from her nose like a big glob of snot.

My little sister hugged a FERRET,
But hugging that ferret did nothing but scare it.
So rather than hug it, she wore it instead
As a soft, fuzzy hat on the top of her head.

My little sister hugged a GOAT,
Which quickly removed its furry coat
And galloped away in its underwear,
Leaving my sister just hugging some hair.

A B C D E F G.
My sister's on a hugging spree!

My little sister hugged a HOG,
Who slipped as it waddled around in a bog
And landed—kerplunk!—with a thunderous thud
On top of my sister in soft, gooey mud.

My little sister hugged an IGUANA.
I can't imagine why she'd wanna.
It almost kissed her, but <u>oops</u>! it missed her
And kissed the poor ferret instead of my sister.

My little sister hugged a JACKAL.
She caught it with a flying tackle.
The jackal was fast, but my sister was faster.
She's a quick little hugger, and nothing gets past her.

She climbed in the pouch of a KANGAROO
And hugged it and all of the babies there, too.
But the kangaroo hopped, and she fell from its pouch
And ended up hugging a pricker bush——ouch!

My little sister hugged a LLAMA
And also its brothers and sisters and mama,
As well as its daddy and uncles and cousins.
Llamas prefer to be hugged by the dozens.

My little sister hugged a MOOSE.
She was hugging its top when its bottom came loose.
She picked up the pieces that fell on the floor
And screwed them together and hugged it some more.

My little sister hugged a NEWT,
Who climbed in her mouth because it looked cute
And crawled so far down that you hardly could spot him.
All you could see sticking out was his bottom.

She gave an OCTOPUS a hug.
Those eight long arms felt nice and snug,
Gripping my sister in eight different spots
And tangling themselves into eight different knots.

And then she hugged a PORCUPINE,
But the long, prickly needles all over its spine
Kept poking the poor little newt in the rear,
Till the newt ran away from my sister in fear.

My little sister hugged a QUAIL,
Who tickled the octopus with its tail.
The poor ticklish octopus laughed till it cried,
And its eight ticklish arms came completely untied.

My little sister hugged a RAT.
She hugged that rat till it was flat.
Then she blew in its ear till it filled up with air
And hugged it again with a little more care.

My little sister hugged a SKUNK,
Which would have been pleasant except that it stunk.
And the rat and the quail and the porcupine, too,
All held their noses and hollered, "Pee-yoo!"

My little sister hugged a TOAD.
"Be careful," it shouted, "or I'll explode!"
So she hugged the toad lightly rather than tightly,
For toads that explode can be rather unsightly.

Next she hugged an UMBRELLA BIRD
But ended up looking a little absurd,
For she hugged it so hard that the bird laid an egg,
Which broke into pieces and ran down her leg.

A B C D E F G
H I J K L M N O P
Q R S T U V.
My sister's on a hugging spree!

My little sister hugged a VOLE,
Who dragged her down its deep, dark hole.
And she probably still would be stuck down there
If the ape hadn't lifted her out by the hair.

My little sister hugged a WORM,
Which might make other people squirm.
Not my sister. It even kissed her!
But a kiss from a worm doesn't bother my sister.

She hugged an X-RAY of a bear.
It was only bones, no skin or hair.
"There's nothing to squeeze," she said with a shrug.
"It crumples right up when I give it a hug."

My little sister hugged a YAK,
Who climbed upon my sister's back,
For the yak was the kind that hugs from behind.
Yaks that hug frontwards are harder to find.

She hugged a young ZEBRA whose paint hadn't dried
And wiped all the stripes from the poor zebra's hide.
The zebra looked silly—its stripes were all gone.
But my sister looked sillier—<u>she</u> had them on!

ABCDEFG
HIJKLMNOP
QRSTUV
WXYZ.
My sister's on a hugging spree!
Oh my gosh! She's hugging . . . ME!